It's five years since ~~~~~~~~~~~~~
transformed into alie~~~~~~ ught
crime with his cousin G~~en and their
Grandpa Max.

Now 15 years old, Ben is once again
forced to turn to the Omnitrix to help
fight a new and more sinister threat
– the HighBreed, DNAliens and the
Forever Knights, who team up to take
over the world.

The watch-like Omnitrix has
re-programmed itself and has a
complete set of ten brand new alien
choices for Ben to get to grips with.
Helped by his cousin Gwen with her
magical powers and Ben's former
enemy, Kevin E. Levin, Ben is soon all
set to go hero once again!

NOW READ ON ...

MEET THE CHARACTERS

Ben Tennyson
Can transform into 10 cool superheroes

Gwen Tennyson
She's Ben's cousin and is sassy and brave

Kevin E. Levin
Helps Ben and Gwen in battle and has absorbing powers

Julie Yamamoto
She goes to school with Ben and he has a crush on her

Brain Storm
Super-brainy and can whip up electromagnetic storms

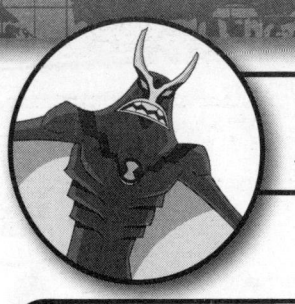

Jet Ray
Can fly and swim faster
than the speed of sound

Humungousaur
He can grow up to
20 metres high

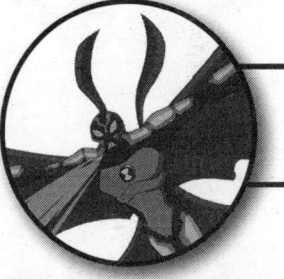

Big Chill
Can turn into an
invisible ghost

Spidermonkey
Can spin deadly webs

Albedo
Out to cause serious
trouble on Earth

Azmuth of the Galvan
The genius that
created the Omnitrix

EGMONT

We bring stories to life

First published in Great Britain 2010
by Egmont UK Limited
239 Kensington High Street,
London W8 6SA

Adapted by Barry Hutchison

ISBN 978 1 4052 5412 0
1 3 5 7 9 10 8 6 4 2

Printed and bound in Great Britain

Egmont is passionate about helping to preserve the world's remaining ancient forests.
We only use paper from legal and sustainable forest sources.

FSC
Mixed Sources
Product group from well-managed
forests and other controlled sources
Cert no. TT-COC-002332
www.fsc.org
© 1996 Forest Stewardship Council

This book is made from paper certified by the Forestry Stewardship Council (FSC),
an organisation dedicated to promoting responsible management of forest resources.
For more information on the FSC, please visit www.fsc.org. To learn more about
Egmont's sustainable paper policy, please visit www.egmont.co.uk/ethical

BEN 10 ALIEN FORCE™

PIER PRESSURE

CHAPTER ONE

THE INVITATION

Fingers of smoke curled up from a deep trench that ran like a scar across the ground. It cut through fences and trees, churned up concrete and soil, before finally coming to an end in the middle of a field.

In the hole at the heart of the field, a damaged spaceship lay still. It was silent, aside from the faint pings made by the metal exterior as it slowly cooled down.

Underneath the ship, a black, oily liquid dripped down onto the ground. For a moment it looked as if the spacecraft had sprung a leak, but then the gloopy liquid squirmed out from beneath the ship, and up the side of the trench.

As the thing crawled along, a pattern of green circles formed on its black surface. The design looked strange and yet to anyone who had ever encountered the alien hero known as Upgrade, it would have looked very familiar.

Wriggling through the grass, the blob came to a busy motorway. Directly across from the field, a truck driver had just finished fixing a flat tyre. He stood back and wiped sweat from his brow.

He was so busy admiring his handiwork that he didn't notice the alien blob sneak up and squeeze through the radiator grille of the truck.

Once inside, the blob began to expand. It oozed across every piece of metal it touched, giving the engine the same black and green pattern as it had.

In just a few seconds the entire lorry was covered with the same design. The driver jumped back in fright when the truck roared noisily into life and sped off along the motorway.

'Hey!' bellowed the driver, giving chase. 'Where you going with my –?'

SCREEECH!

The lorry's brakes locked on, sending the entire vehicle into a sharp spin. When it was facing towards the driver again it lurched forwards, smoke pouring from the exhaust.

The driver stumbled backwards, shielding his face with his hands even though he knew it would do him no good. Through his fingers he spied something unbelievable. As the truck sped towards him it started changing. The entire engine bay split in two, opening up like a giant mouth.

The last thing the driver saw before closing his eyes was the mechanical mouth opening wider, revealing row after row of deadly green-and-black teeth!

Ben and Gwen were sat in the middle of a crowd of people, their heads turning left then right then left then right. An inter-school tennis match was taking place. A girl from Ben's school – Julie Yamamoto – was playing a girl from another school. It was a close game, but Julie had just edged into the lead.

As Julie got ready to serve, she spotted Ben. A smile spread across her face. She gave him a wave, before turning back to the game.

An even bigger smile broke out across Ben's face. Gwen couldn't help but notice. 'She waved. She likes you. You should ask her out.'

Ben blushed and looked down. 'No way. What if she finds out about the Omnitrix? I don't want her to think I'm weird.'

'Ben, you are weird,' Gwen pointed out. 'But you're also funny and sensitive and well-mannered. Unlike some people I know.'

Gwen turned around and looked behind her. Kevin was sprawled out across two chairs. His head was back and he was snoring loudly.

Suddenly, the crowd erupted in cheers as Julie hammered a shot past her opponent. Ben and Gwen leapt up, punching the air in delight. From behind them they heard Kevin splutter.

'What'd I miss?'

'She won!' said Ben, happily.

'Go ahead, Ben!' said Gwen, giving her cousin a friendly nudge. 'Now's your chance!'

'Uh, I'm not sure ... aaghh!' Ben's sentence was cut short by Gwen pulling him down the steps towards the court.

Julie had just finished shaking hands

with her opponent when Gwen shoved Ben towards her.

'Whoa!' Ben yelped, stumbling and almost falling at Julie's feet.

'Ben!' beamed Julie, pleased to see him.

'Julie, hey!' Ben replied, nervously.

'Good game, Julie!' said Gwen. She gave her cousin a pointed look. 'Ben?'

'Right, way to go,' Ben stammered. 'Great game. Match. Set. Whatever.' He swallowed hard, knowing what he wanted to say, but too afraid to say it. 'Well, see ya.'

Flashing another nervous smile, he turned on the spot, only for Gwen to catch him by the elbow and spin him back round.

'Back so soon?' asked Julie, grinning.

'Heh, so, um, Julie? I was wondering if you'd like to, I dunno, get together. Sometime.'

'Sure. When?'

Ben spun around to face his cousin, his eyes wide with panic. 'She said "when?". That's like a yes, only more specific,' he whispered. 'Now what?'

'You say, "how about tonight?".'

Ben's face went pale. 'Tonight?' he said, in a voice that was barely more than a squeak. Gwen nodded, and so Ben turned back to Julie, trying to act as naturally as possible. 'Ahem, I mean, we could go to the pier. Tonight.'

Julie nodded. 'Great!'

Ben stood there, nodding and smiling, not entirely sure what he should say next.

'Well,' began Julie at last. 'Guess I'll hit

the showers.'

'Yes!' cried Ben, relieved not to have to think of something to say. 'Good. Me too. I mean, er ... '

'He'll come by around seven,' said Gwen, stepping in to save her cousin from embarrassing himself even more. 'Sometimes I wonder,' she muttered, as she dragged him towards the exit, 'how the species survives.'

A few miles away, a policeman stood by the side of the road, looking down at the wreckage of an eighteen-wheeler truck. He spoke into his radio.

'Yeah, I found that stolen truck. No, no sign of whoever took it.'

Behind the officer, a squidgy black and green blob squirmed over to his police car and climbed inside it. In moments, the alien pattern had swept over the entire vehicle.

'Whaddya mean, "he says it drove away by itself"?' snorted the policeman in reply to someone on the other end of the radio. 'That just doesn't happen.'

VROOOM! The police car's engine roared loudly.

' ... much,' added the policeman, flatly, as he watched his car speed off into the distance.

Ben stared at his reflection in his bedroom mirror. He was not pleased with what he saw.

'Great. My hair looks stupid, my shirt is wrinkled, and I have a zit the size of Kansas.'

'Yeah, that's one big zit alright.'

Ben wheeled around to find Kevin standing behind him, grinning.

'How did you get in here?'

'The usual way,' replied Kevin, holding up a fist. It shone like polished metal. 'You may want to fix that hole I punched in your back door before your mother sees it.'

Ben sighed. 'You couldn't knock?'

'I sort of did.'

'Has anyone ever told you that you're a strange and dangerous person?' asked Ben.

'Constantly. But enough about me. Gwen says you need a favour.'

'Uh, yeah. See, I kinda want to go to the

pier tonight with Julie.'

'I bet you do,' smirked Kevin.

'And since I don't have a car –'

'Or a license,' Kevin reminded him.

'Or a license,' Ben nodded. He hesitated. Why was he even bothering to ask? There was no way Kevin would agree to it. 'Well, so I was wondering if you could, um, maybe give us a ride to the pier?'

For a moment Kevin said nothing. Finally, he shrugged his shoulders. 'OK.'

Ben's eyes went wide with surprise. 'That's it? No jokes, no insults, no blackmail?'

'Nope.'

'Wow. Thanks,' began Ben, before a thought occurred to him. 'Wait. You're gonna wait till we're in the car and then you're going to make my life miserable, aren't you?'

A wicked smile spread across Kevin's face, but he didn't say anything as he turned and walked out of the bedroom.

'This should be fun,' Ben muttered, before setting off after Kevin, ready for his date with Julie.

CHAPTER TWO

CAR TROUBLE

Kevin's car cut through the early-evening traffic on the way to the pier. Gwen sat in the front passenger seat, with Ben and Julie sitting in the back.

'Now remember, little Benny boy,' said Kevin, in the voice of a controlling dad he'd once seen in a television show, 'your mother and I want you home by ten o'clock sharp, or you can't go to the disco!'

Julie blinked, confused. 'Disco?'

Ben shook his head, indicating she should ignore Kevin. 'He watches a lot of repeats,' he explained.

'Give him a break, Kevin,' said Gwen.

'Gosh, pumpkin, what do you mean?' Kevin asked, still using the same goofy voice.

'You know exactly what I mean,' Gwen

whispered. 'At least when Ben likes a girl he lets her know. He asks her out. Maturity, isn't that a novel approach?'

Kevin thought about this for a moment, before launching into song. 'Ben's got a girlfriend, Ben's got a girlfriend!'

Ben groaned loudly as Kevin continued to sing. Neither of them noticed the police car cruising along the street just thirty or so metres behind them – or the fact that it had nobody behind the wheel.

When Ben and Julie stepped out of Kevin's car, they had no idea they were being watched. Further along the street, the green-and-black police car was doing its best to hide behind a lamppost. Its headlights blinked like eyes as it watched Kevin's car drive away, and saw Ben and Julie stroll onto the pier.

The pier itself was a fairground-type attraction, with games, rides and stalls filling every available space. On some nights it was almost impossible to move for people. Tonight was not one of those nights.

'Listen, uh, sorry about Kevin,' muttered Ben, as he and Julie walked along.

'Why is he so mean to you?'

'It makes him happy.'

Julie giggled. 'You're nice to let him.'

Ben smiled and looked around properly

for the first time. 'Slow night. This place is packed on weekends.'

'Good,' said Julie, brightly. She slipped her arm through Ben's. 'This way we have the place to ourselves.'

'Yeah,' said Ben, smiling from ear to ear. 'Guess we do.'

BE-DEEP! BE-DEEP! BE-DEEP!

Ben stared down at the Omnitrix. It was emitting a high-pitched screeching sound he'd never heard it make before.

'Is that a watch?' Julie asked, stepping back and covering her ears.

'Heh, yeah,' Ben replied. 'Really have to get it fixed. You like candy floss?' he asked, then spoke again before she had a chance to reply. 'Good, you stay here, I'll be back!'

Without another word, he turned and ran off between two stalls, leaving Julie alone, and a little confused.

When he was safely out of sight, Ben gave the Omnitrix a shake, trying to make it shut up. 'Typical,' he muttered. 'Everything's going great then this freaks out on me.'

Over by the entrance to the pier, the green-and-black blob slithered onto the boardwalk. It's alien sensors locked onto Ben and the Omnitrix immediately, and for a moment it just sat there, watching the boy shake the watch violently up and down.

At last the blob turned and fixed its gaze on the bumper cars, where some people were having fun crashing into one another. Moving as quickly as its slug-like body would allow, the blob crawled towards the dodgems.

Ben, meanwhile, was trying another technique with the Omnitrix. He was slamming it against the wooden stall he was hiding behind. On the fifth smack, the alarm fell silent.

'That's more like it,' said Ben, quietly, before a panicked scream from the bumper car ride shattered his new-found silence.

Ben looked up to see a bumper car leaping over the barrier surrounding the ride. It thudded down onto the wooden pier, then barrelled towards him, its one headlight blazing like the eye of a Cyclops.

The sparkling lights of the fair reflected off the shiny green-and-black surface of the car as it reared up so it stood as tall as Ben himself. Then, to Ben's surprise and horror, a wide gap appeared in the car's surface, just below the headlight. The gap widened, revealing several large and lethal-looking teeth.

As the shadow of the bumper car passed over him, Ben swallowed hard, 'That seriously cannot be good.'

The car lurched closer and closer and Ben had to dodge sideways to avoid being splattered. Turning, he ran from the car, powering along the deserted pier as fast as his legs would carry him.

Over the thudding of his footsteps Ben heard another sound. An electric engine revved and whined behind him, getting louder as the dodgem drew nearer. He wanted to look back over his shoulder to see how close the car was, but to do that would mean slowing down, and slowing down seemed like a very bad idea.

Ben came to a corner where the rows of sideshows ran off in another direction. Catching the side of one of the stalls he swung himself around without slowing. He heard the squeal of brakes and felt the pier shudder as the bumper car skidded and crashed into the wall of a shop.

Still Ben ran. Bumper cars were built for crashing. There was no way a little collision like that would slow this one down.

Sure enough, just a few seconds later Ben heard the whine of the engine once again. Tucking his head down he pushed himself to go faster, ignoring the burning pain in his legs.

A candy floss stand seemed to loom up

out of nowhere, right in Ben's path. Too close to go around it, Ben could only leap up onto the stand and hurl himself off the other side. The candy floss seller ducked as Ben came bounding over the top of him.

'Watch it!' he cried, angrily.

KA-RUNCH!

The bumper car clipped the corner of the cart, sending it into a spin. The candy floss seller yelped as he was knocked down onto his bottom on the hard wooden pier. He eyed his damaged cart as it slowly stopped spinning. Someone would have to pay for this – and he knew just who to blame!

Thirty metres away, the car skidded around another corner and stopped. The part of the pattern that looked most like a face pulled into a frown as the vehicle's alien scanners searched for Ben. They panned left and right, sweeping over the entire area, but could find no trace of him anywhere.

Way up high, almost directly above the bumper car, Ben clung tightly to the side of a tall ride. He watched the car below, hardly daring to even breathe. 'What is this?' he whispered. 'When Carnival Rides Attack?'

At the back of the bumper car a long metal pole – usually used to connect to the electrical circuit that powers the dodgems – began to glow an eerie shade of blue. As Ben looked on, circles of green light rose from the tip of the pole. Ben almost lost his grip when he guessed what was happening. The dodgem car was sending out some kind of homing signal. And that meant –

BE-DEEP! BE-DEEP! BE-DEEP!

Once again the Omnitrix emitted a piercing alarm.

'Ssh!' Ben urged, releasing his grip for long enough to give the watch a sharp shake. But the alarm continued, and from up on the side of the ride Ben saw the bumper car twist to look in his direction.

VROOM!

The dodgem sprung forwards, its wheels spraying smoke. Ben braced himself, gripping on tightly as the car raced straight towards the ride he was clinging to.

The front of the bumper car struck the metal structure, sending vibrations all the way to the top. Despite all his efforts, Ben's fingers weren't strong enough to hold on. He toppled backwards, his arms reaching out, clawing at the air as he fought to find something to catch on to.

It was no use. Screaming, Ben fell away from the carnival ride and plummeted backwards towards the ground below.

CHAPTER THREE

EL MATADOR

WHUUMP!

Ben landed hard in the passenger seat of the bumper car. He wasn't sure if this was good news or bad news. It was good that he hadn't splattered onto the ground, but now he was at the mercy of the possessed car, which had begun to race along the pier the second he had landed. Still, at least the Omnitrix had stopped screaming at him. For now.

The speed of the car made the wind sting Ben's eyes as he stood up in the seat. 'OK,' he said, fixing his gaze on a rope that was strung across the boardwalk up ahead, 'I am so over this!'

Hurling himself into the air, Ben caught hold of the rope and swung upwards. The bumper car accelerated beneath him, leaving him behind. Ben dropped silently down onto the wooden pier and whipped off his jacket. If the car wanted a fight, he'd give it one!

'Hey, bumpo, bumpo!' he cried, twirling his jacket around like a bull-fighter's cape. The bumper car skidded around so it was facing him and immediately began to charge.

The whine of the electric motor grew louder and louder in Ben's ears. The car was already almost upon him, but he couldn't move yet. He had to hold his nerve for just a few seconds more ...

Now!

Ben whipped the jacket away at the last possible second, revealing a solid metal post bolted to a concrete block that was set into the floor of the pier. The car had no time to stop, no chance of avoiding the head-on crash.

The car folded around the metal pole as if its bonnet were made of modelling clay. While the front half of the dodgem stopped instantly, the back end kept on going, collapsing the entire vehicle in on itself.

As Ben watched, the green-and-black pattern that had been covering the car faded away, returning the vehicle to its original colour, if not its original shape.

'I hope there's a simple explanation for this,' Ben said. 'But I doubt it.'

A sharp squeaking sound from his left made Ben turn. The candy floss seller limped along the pier, dragging his badly damaged cart behind him. The man did not look in the slightest bit happy.

'Kid, you and me got a date with my insurance adjuster,' he growled.

A jolt of panic shot through Ben. 'Date!' he cried. 'Aaaah!'

Reaching into the cart, Ben grabbed two sticks of candy floss. 'Look, here's my allowance,' he said, handing the salesman a ten dollar bill. 'It's all I've got.'

'And then he ran off,' said Julie, speaking into her mobile phone, 'and I've been ... wait, he's coming back. Later.'

Ben clattered to a halt beside her, out of breath from running so far.

'Sorry,' he panted. 'You would not believe that queue.'

Julie glanced around. 'Ben, there's nobody here.'

'Um, except at the concession stand, where they've been doing huge business,' replied Ben, smiling a little too broadly.

'I thought you'd stood me up,' said Julie, glancing down at her feet.

Ben looked shocked. 'Julie,' he said, 'I'd never, ever do that to you.'

He held out the candy floss and smiled again – for real this time. 'Look, I got pink and blue. Your pick.'

A smile crept across Julie's face and she took the pink stick. She picked some off and popped it in her mouth, while Ben opened his jaws and chomped down on a huge piece of his own candy floss. She giggled when he opened his mouth again, revealing two rows of bright blue teeth.

Ben gave a faint sigh of relief. Maybe this date wouldn't be a complete disaster after all.

A few miles away, in a deep crater in a dark field, a solitary figure shuffled around the fallen spaceship.

Ping. Ping. Ping. Ping.

A warning light blinked on a control panel, slow at first, but gradually becoming faster and louder. The figure hobbled closer and reached a hand out to touch the panel.

'Aaaaaargh!' he howled in pain as ribbons of electric-blue energy wrapped around his hand and danced up his arm.

Anyone crossing the field would have heard the cries and seen the flickering blue glow of the electricity. But there was no-one crossing the field. No-one to see the light or hear the cries.

The figure in the ship was alone. Alone and screaming in the darkness.

Julie and Ben stood at the foot of some metal stairs, looking up at a full-sized replica of an F-15 fighter jet. The jet was fixed in place by a large metal pole. It moved up and down, left and right, making the fighter plane buck and thrash around.

'This looks fun,' said Julie.

'Especially if you don't mind wrenching G-forces and waves of nausea,' said Ben, nodding enthusiastically.

Julie laughed. 'Are you saying you don't want to ride it?'

'No, I'm saying it's a good thing I didn't get us cheeseburgers!' said Ben, before a movement on the surface of the aeroplane caught his attention. The shiny silver surface of one wing was taking on the black-and-green appearance. It was the same pattern he'd seen on the bumper car, and that could only mean one thing ... trouble.

'Uh-oh.'

'You OK?' asked Julie.

'Me? Fine. No problem,' said Ben, quickly. 'Listen, maybe we should skip this one?'

'Ben Tennyson, are you hiding something?' Julie teased.

'No, no secrets here,' Ben babbled, 'my

life's an open book, just your basic regular guy.'

The alien pattern finished covering the jet fighter, and the entire ride rippled like the surface of a lake. With a sudden burst of flame from its engines, the giant model aeroplane rose up and tilted so its nose was pointed directly at the couple.

'Here we go again,' Ben groaned.

The jet made a lunge for Ben, clamping its wings shut almost as if it were clapping a pair of enormous hands. The metal slammed together just centimetres from Ben's head, making Julie scream with fright. Ben caught her by the arm and dragged her away from the ride, shouting, 'This way!'

They hurried along the boardwalk, Ben in front, Julie being pulled along behind him. Ducking behind a wooden hut, Ben yanked open the door and pushed Julie inside.

'You stay here for a minute.'

'Where are you going?'

Ben hesitated. 'Uh, bathroom?'

Julie was about to say something but Ben didn't give her the chance. Slamming the door closed he pulled up his sleeve and turned the dial on the Omnitrix.

'This looks like a job for Jet Ray!'

CHAPTER FOUR

ALL THE FUN OF THE FAIR

A split-second before Ben could activate the Omnitrix, the jet fighter tore free from its support and screamed over his head. As Ben fell to the floor, he slammed his hand down on the watch.

The transformation began. Six legs sprouted out of his body. Two giant crab pincers appeared where his arms had been.

'Hey, this isn't Jet Ray,' Ben said, then quickly realising that he was thinking more clearly than ever before. 'Brain Storm!'

THWACK!

The jet fighter swooped down low, catching the crab-alien with a glancing blow to the top of his shell. Brain Storm flipped over and rolled clumsily along the pier, his claws clattering against the wood.

'Now,' he seethed when he finally tumbled to a stop on the boardwalk, 'I am most decidedly miffed.'

The entire top section of the alien's shell unfolded, revealing a bulging pink brain. Sparks bristled on the brain's surface, before coming together to form a funnel of devastating energy.

The first shot tore past the jet fighter, scorching the air just to its left. A second blast found its target, burning a hole clean through one of the aeroplane's wings.

For a moment the plane looked like it

was going down, before jets of flame from its afterburners pulled it around in a loop-the-loop.

Brain Storm stopped firing and watched as the plane banked down towards him. A strange green glow lit up the tips of its wings. 'What the deuce?' the crab-alien wondered aloud, before bolts of green energy began raining down on him from above.

Shutting his eyes, Brain Storm managed to throw up a force field around himself. The jet fighter's energy bolts bounced off the shield, striking surrounding huts instead.

The door to one hut creaked open and Julie poked her head out. She could hardly believe what she saw. A giant crab was standing a few metres away, and a jet fighter was firing something directly towards her!

A shimmering force field suddenly encased Julie, protecting her from the blasts of green energy which tore through the hut.

As Brain Storm's force field carried Julie to safety, the jet fighter's scanners locked on to her, analysing her from head to toe. When its scan was complete the plane rolled in mid-air and banked sharply towards the farthest end of the pier, where Julie was now standing unprotected.

KZAAAAP!

A coil of energy blasted from within Brain Storm's brain, almost splitting the jet in half. Its engines died instantly. Pouring smoke from its tail-end, the plane nose-dived down onto the pier.

In pieces it slid along the wooden planks, throwing up sparks as it hurtled towards the metal safety barrier. Before it hit the barrier, its wings clipped a towering swing ride, bringing the whole structure down on top of it.

Tangled together, the jet and the carnival ride smashed through the safety barrier and plunged down into the icy cold water below.

Brain Storm gave a satisfied nod. 'And good riddance, might I say?'

A few moments and a quick transformation later, Ben emerged from the men's bathroom and raced to find Julie.

'Did I miss anything?' he asked.

'You didn't see that?' spluttered Julie.

'See what?'

With a thunderous splash, the swing ride

rose up from the water behind Ben, the alien pattern covering every part of it.

'Erm, that!' cried Julie, pointing upwards.

The structure loomed like a giant robot, the swinging seat pods attached to each of its four metal arms poised like huge fists, ready to smash down. Before Ben could fully understand what he was seeing, one of the fists swung down at him. Instinctively he ducked. Julie, however, wasn't so lucky.

'Ben!' she screamed, as the seating cage snapped shut around her, trapping her inside. She screamed for a second time when the ride lurched suddenly upwards, lifting her high above the pier.

Moving unsteadily, the living fairground ride stepped up onto the boardwalk. Ben felt the pier bend beneath him. He threw himself sideways, trying to make it to safety before –

SNAP!

The boards around him broke and he felt the world lurch sickeningly to one side. He threw his hands out, reaching for something – anything – that would help slow his fall.

His fingers found something solid. He looked up and discovered he was holding onto the edge of a broken plank. He didn't dare look down at the swirling waters beneath him.

Above the screams of the people on the pier, Ben heard Julie shouting his name. The carnival ride was stomping off through the water, towards the outskirts of the city.

Ben looked at the Omnitrix. He was holding on with his other hand, meaning he didn't have any fingers free to activate the watch. As the giant robot marched further away, and Julie's cries became fainter and fainter, Ben shook his head in despair.

'This,' he said, 'is just not my night.'

And with that, he let go, barely leaving himself enough time to gulp down a deep breath before he plunged beneath the surface of the water.

Unseen by anyone on the pier, a flash of green Omnitrix energy lit up the waves. A moment later Jet Ray leapt out of the water and soared upwards, like a mutant flying fish.

'None of this makes sense,' he muttered, 'Why am I being attacked by carnival rides? And why'd it grab Julie?'

Cars weaved out of the way, horns blaring, as the mutant swing ride thundered along the motorway.

Above it all, Jet Ray glided in, working on a plan as he surveyed the scene.

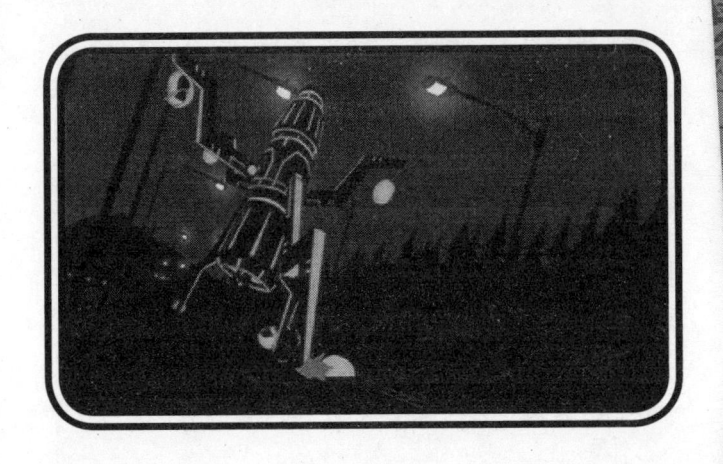

He spotted some lampposts up ahead.
Firing his energy blasts, Jet Ray brought two
of the metal poles toppling down across the
road directly in front of the carnival ride. The
lampposts caught on one of its mechanical feet,
forcing it to stop.

The sudden halt sent its arms flailing
wildly, forcing Julie to cling to the safety bar
across her lap to avoid being thrown out. Jet
Ray flew towards her, trying to reach her before
the swing ride realised what was going on.

Too late!

Another of the pods tumbled through the sky and hit Jet Ray hard. He crashed down to Earth, buried beneath the twisted metal.

Jet Ray's claws made short work of the pod, and in just a few seconds he was back up. But there was one small problem. The carnival ride was gone.

And so was Julie.

CHAPTER FIVE

THE SHIPS

Jet Ray rocketed towards the sky, spinning around and around, searching for any sign of the mechanical monster and –

There! The swing ride was racing through a forest, heading in the direction of a field. From up high, Jet Ray could see the deep trench cut into the field, but that didn't matter right now. Only one thing mattered. Julie.

Soaring on his leathery wings, Jet Ray gave chase. By the time he caught up with the runaway ride, it was squatting in the middle of the field by the end of the trench. Julie, however, was nowhere to be seen.

'What have you done with Julie?' Jet Ray snarled.

'I'm here!' Julie stepped out from behind one of the swing-ride's legs, brushing dust from her clothes. 'And how do you know my name?'

Oops. How was he going to talk his way out of this one? There was only one thing for it. It was time for the truth, even if that did make her think he was a freak.

'Julie, don't be scared,' Jet Ray said, landing softly in front of her. 'It's me. It's Ben. I'm not going to hurt you.'

'You're a monster?' Julie gasped.

'No. Well, yes,' Jet Ray admitted. 'Actually, I'm like ten monsters.'

The alien hung his head, too ashamed to look at her.

'Cool!'

Jet Ray raised his eyes to see Julie smiling. In a flash he transformed back to Ben. 'Cool?' he repeated, stepping closer.

Before Julie could answer, the fairground ride loomed over them and began to emit high-pitched squeals. The sounds changed, before becoming something resembling a human voice.

'Ship ship ship ship ship!' it said.

'Excuse me, we're talking,' Ben said.

'I think it's trying to tell you something.'

The ride nudged Ben with the side of its foot. 'Ship ship ship,' it chirped.

Shifting its weight to the side, the ride pointed to the trench, where the alien craft lay.

'Ship. You've brought us out here to find that spaceship,' Ben realised. 'Right?'

He glanced up at the swing ride in time to see the black-and-green pattern fade away, revealing the original colours beneath. Slowly, the metal frame collapsed.

Ben clambered down into the trench and edged closer to the spacecraft. A large hole had been torn in one side, and through it he could see a familiar-looking alien figure trapped beneath some fallen machinery.

'I've seen that thing before,' he said.

'You have?' Julie frowned.

'Kinda. I ... used to be able to turn into one of those. Called myself "Upgrade".'

The alien gave a whimper of pain.

'Well whatever it is, it's hurt,' said Julie, moving towards the ship. She stopped when Ben held his arm out. He nodded towards the faint red glow surrounding the spacecraft.

'You get any closer to that energy field and it'll fry you like a potato,' he warned.

Julie nodded and peered inside the ship. A monitor displayed a series of strange alien symbols. Each one flashed red on the screen.

'What's that say?'

'Sorry, I don't read alien,' Ben confessed.

Down by his leg, Ben felt something bump against him. He looked down to find a black-and-green blob nudging him on the shin. 'So you're what's behind all this?' he said.

'Ship!' yelped the little alien goo-ball.

Ben shrugged. 'OK. "Ship".'

Ship wriggled backwards. With a ripple of its gloopy body, it moulded itself into the shape of the crashed spacecraft. Julie was about to applaud when the miniature version of the spaceship exploded in a shower of goo.

As Ship pulled himself back together, Julie turned to Ben. 'OK, now I know he's trying to tell you something!'

'It's a countdown,' Ben gasped, watching the symbols on the monitor count down. 'That thing's gonna explode!'

There was no time to waste. Slapping the Omnitrix, Ben transformed himself into the mighty Humungousaur and thundered towards the damaged vessel.

Pulling aside debris, Humungousaur found the cause of the problem. A damaged engine core hung from its housing. Its energy coils had been exposed, triggering a meltdown.

Moving quickly, the dino-alien ripped the engine core free and hurled it skyward.

BADOOOOOOM!

The engine core went off like a bomb. Sparks shot like fireworks in all directions.

Humungousaur knelt down and wrapped his arms around Julie, cradling her protectively until long after the blast had died away.

'Um, explosion's over,' said Julie, smiling.

Humungousaur released her and stood up. 'Right,' he muttered. Even through his thick orange skin, there was no way for the dino-alien to hide the fact that he was blushing!

'There you go,' said Humungousaur, lifting the fallen equipment from the alien pilot.

'Yes. Well, as I was saying,' began
the pilot, getting to his feet. 'I extruded this
symbiont, the one you call "Ship" –'

'Ship! Ship!' chattered the blob.

'I sent it off to find the nearest Plumber.'

Julie frowned. 'Because your sink was
clogged?'

'Plumbers are intergalactic police
officers,' Humungousaur told her. 'I'll explain
later.' He turned back to the alien. 'And that's
why it came after me?'

'Of course. Didn't you receive its signal?'

'You mean the beeping?'

'Yes, the "beeping",' the pilot grimaced. 'Don't you know how the Omnitrix works?'

'Not so much. No.'

'Really?' asked the pilot, surprised. 'Aren't you a Plumber?'

'No, I thought you were.'

'Spend the rest of my life here?' the alien muttered to himself, shuddering at the thought. 'Look, is there anyone else I can talk with?'

'Not really.'

'That's why Ship tried to get your attention.'

Green light flickered as Humungousaur changed back to Ben. 'Get my attention? He wrecked the pier! He kidnapped Julie!'

'Well, I needed help,' sniffed the pilot.

'That's pretty obvious,' Ben replied.

'And you wonder why most aliens only communicate with your livestock,' the pilot grumbled. 'Now, I must repair my warp drive.'

Julie flashed a friendly smile. 'Anything we can do to help?'

Hours later, Ben and Julie were doing their best to reattach an antenna to the ship.

'There, it's on tight,' said Julie, proudly.

Ben nodded, 'I, uh, I guess this is probably the worst date you've ever had, huh?'

'No. Just different,' Julie replied, resting a hand on his arm. 'And being different is fine.'

A hatch swung open between them.
'Right. All done,' announced the pilot. 'Off I go.'

Ben and Julie hopped down, almost
landing on Ship, who was rolling in the dirt.

'What about this thing?' asked Ben.
'Doesn't he blorp back into your body?'

'That's not how it works. Besides,
you and he have had such a lovely bonding
experience. He's yours now.'

Ben and Julie watched the alien craft
rise into the air and streak off towards the
far reaches of outer space. They turned their
attention down to the blob by Ben's side.

'He's cute,' Julie teased. 'Are you going to keep him?'

Ben didn't answer. There was too much going on in his head at that moment for him to find words. He knew they had a long walk to get back to town. He knew they would both be in big trouble with their parents, but despite all that – despite everything that had happened at the pier – Ben couldn't help but think that tonight had been the best night of his life!

'Come on,' he said, looking from Julie to Ship and back again. 'Let's go home.'

A possessed bumper car
crashes Ben's date

Time to use some serious
brainpower!

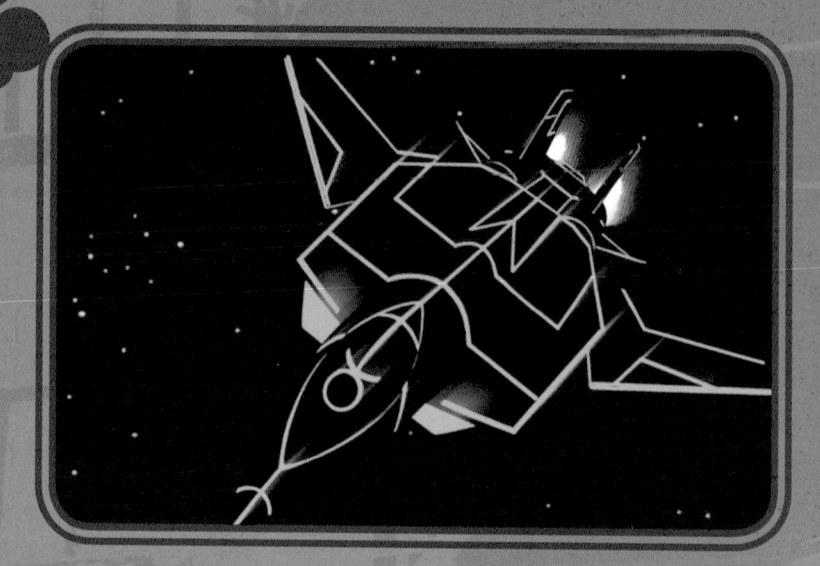

A fairground ride turns
into a rocket

Then Julie goes for a ride
in the sky

Jet Ray flexes his awesome wings

Then he has some
explaining to do!

The strange ship lands
in the woods

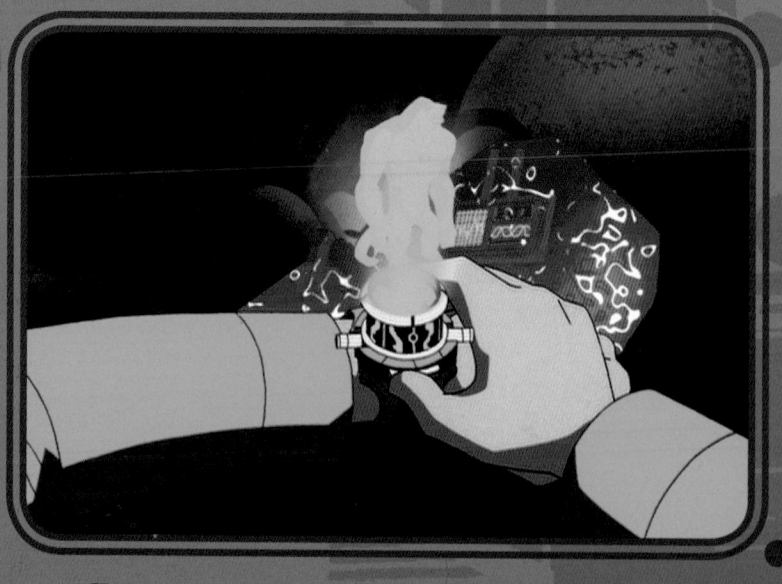

Ben turns into Humungousaur!

A strange being
transforms into Ben

Humungousaur and Jet Ray
prepare for an all-out battle!

Gwen uses a magic stone
to locate the evil imposter

Then Big Chill fires an ice-cold
blast at Swampfire

Jet Ray fires burning lasers at Echo Echo

Gwen and Kevin are left hanging around

Now it's Big Chill's turn
to get blasted

But Azmuth of the Galvan shows
the gang who's boss!

GOOD COPY, BAD COPY

CHAPTER ONE

DOUBLE TROUBLE

CLANK. CLANK. CLANK.

Running in armour wasn't easy, but the Forever Knights were trying their best. They barged into each other, tripping and stumbling as they hurried across a heavy wooden drawbridge which hung above a moat of churning lava.

Behind them, the thing chasing them drew steadily closer.

Into their castle they scurried, shouting, screaming for the drawbridge to be raised. With a grinding of gears and a clatter of chains, the solid oak bridge was quickly pulled up into position, blocking the huge doorway and preventing the evil monster outside from getting inside.

BOOM!

Something powerful slammed hard against the wood.

BOOOM!

The Forever Knights huddled together closely, all drawing their swords and saying their prayers.

BOOOOOM!

The drawbridge and part of the wall exploded inwards, showering the knights with splinters of wood and fragments of stone. Someone near the front of the group wailed with terror as he finally caught sight of the creature that had chased them here.

The whole castle shook as Humungousaur pushed his way into the entrance hallway. He had grown so large that he had to duck to avoid hitting his head on the ceiling. Knights fell before him like skittles as he rushed forwards, flicking his thick tail from side to side.

Across the room, one knight caught the dino-alien's eye. He was running away at speed, making his way towards another exit at the back of the hall.

Humungousaur was on him in three huge steps. He lashed out with a hand, knocking the knight hard against a moss-covered wall. The knight's armour saved him from being too badly injured, but the blow still hurt. A lot. With a groan, he dropped to his knees.

A hand that was almost the same size as he was caught him around the waist and lifted him into the air. The knight felt another jolt shake his body as he was slammed against the wall again. This time, though, he was held firmly in place.

'Answer me,' demanded Humungousaur, growling even more savagely than he usually did. 'Where is he?'

Behind his metal visor, the knight was quaking with terror. 'Why ask what you already know?' he whimpered. 'Are you testing us?'

Humungousaur leaned in close enough for the knight to feel the heat of his breath, even through the armour. 'I test your will to live,' Humungousaur snarled angrily. 'Now, for the last time ...'

With a sudden flash of green, the alien transformed back into human form. A very familiar boy with brown hair and green eyes stood in Humungousaur's place. The corners of his mouth curled into a wicked smirk as he said, '... where is Ben Tennyson?'

A green and black car prowled slowly along a deserted motorway, its headlights shining like eyes in the darkness. Behind the wheel, Kevin Levin gritted his teeth and tried to ignore the ... weirdness happening in the passenger seat.

Gwen Tennyson sat there – but Kevin certainly had no problem with that. It was the way her eyes were glowing bright pink that made him a little uneasy. And the way that same pink energy was flowing over the surface of the crushed drink can in Gwen's hand.

'Tracking Ben like this feels really weird, Kevin,' Gwen said, her gaze not moving from the glowing can.

'Hey, it was your idea,' Kevin reminded her. 'All I know is there's a lot of alien communication traffic and Tennyson's name keeps coming up.'

'Hang on, I think I'm getting something,' said Gwen, suddenly. The can seemed to pull her hands towards the driver's side of the car. 'Quickly, make a left,' she instructed. 'There's something round that corner.'

Kevin spun the steering wheel and the back end of the car swung sharply out into the road. Pressing down on the accelerator, he powered the car up a steep slope to where a large building loomed in the late-evening gloom.

It was a castle. A castle with a hole where the door should have been.

'Wow,' muttered Gwen, as Kevin skidded the car to a halt less than a metre from the castle's moat. They stood for a moment, staring in amazement at the damage that had been inflicted on the castle.

As well as the hole in the wall, large parts of the roof had caved in. Flames spat up through the gaps, sending clouds of choking grey smoke rolling up towards the sky.

Kevin's eyes followed the smoke, until he spotted a familiar red and yellow figure flying just above the flames. It was Jet Ray, one of the alien forms stored in Ben's Omnitrix.

'Gwen! Up there!'

Gwen followed Kevin's gaze, then cupped her hands to her mouth and shouted, 'Ben! Hey!'

If Jet Ray heard her, he didn't show it. Instead he kept flying, higher and higher, until he was swallowed by the clouds.

For a long time neither of them spoke.

Surely Ben had heard Gwen shouting? Why didn't he turn back?

A low groan of pain drifted over to them from behind a pile of rubble. Gwen and Kevin darted over and peered behind the mound of rocks. There, in the centre of a giant dinosaur footprint, lay a Forever Knight. His armour was dented and scuffed, and Gwen could only imagine how bruised he must be underneath it.

'Ben 10 has shown no mercy,' the knight moaned.

'Well, what did you do?' asked Gwen, certain the knights must have done something to deserve such a beating.

'Nothing, I swear on my order,' the armoured man said. 'He's ruined three of our castles in as many days.'

Kevin and Gwen glanced at each other and shrugged.

'First I've heard of it,' said Gwen.

The knight broke out in a fit of coughing

which shook his entire body. When he was finished, he spoke again. 'They say at court that the cursed Ben 10 has even attacked a hive of DNAliens.'

'Your cousin took out a whole hive?' Kevin snorted at Gwen. 'Come on. He doesn't have the guts.'

'You mean it's not like Ben to go on a mission like that alone,' said Gwen. She chewed her lip nervously and glanced up to the clouds high above. 'Why's he keeping secrets from us?'

Ben stared down at the jumble of numbers on the page in front of him. It didn't make sense. Not one bit of it.

'You get it, Ben?' asked Julie, Ben's friend from school and one of the few people who knew his secret. They were sitting in his bedroom, studying for a science exam. Ben would have given anything to be out fighting aliens instead. At least he understood how to fight aliens.

Julie spotted Ben's blank look and skimmed over the question again. 'The kid weighs twenty-five kilograms,' she began, picking up a handful of chilli fries from a wrapper on Ben's bed and popping one into her mouth. 'Three metres per second, two metres from the edge of the merry-go-round,' she continued, chewing.

Ben quickly wiped the chilli sauce from his own hands and snatched up a pencil. 'Wait, Julie, wait. I'd better write this down.'

A movement by the door caught Julie's eye. She leaned back and looked past Ben to where Kevin and Gwen had entered.

'Congratulations, Tennyson,' Kevin said, grinning from ear to ear. 'You're finally putting the Omnitrix to maximum use. You know, clandestine butt-kicking wise.'

Ben stuffed some more fries in his mouth. 'What are you talking about?'

'Nice try,' said Gwen. 'We saw you as Jet Ray, flying away from a battle.'

Ben looked from Gwen to Kevin and back again, wondering if this was the build up to some kind of joke. 'Look, I've been studying all week for a physics test tomorrow. It's my worst subject.'

Gwen raised an eyebrow. 'Maybe you're not really studying.'

'Wait,' said Julie, cutting in. 'Considering the aliens and weird transformations and stuff Ben deals with, there could be any number of explanations for what you saw.'

'You saying you can vouch for his whereabouts?' asked Kevin.

Julie hesitated. 'No. I got here a few minutes ago,' she confessed. 'He studies, then I come over to help him review.' She glanced down at the mess of scribbles in Ben's notebook. 'Not that he's acing the reviews.'

'I'm getting better!' Ben protested.

Julie patted him on the arm. 'You're making a real effort.'

'With Grandpa Max gone, we've got to rely on each other,' said Gwen. She fixed Ben with a serious stare. 'If you've got a secret you should spill it. Now.'

Ben held one hand over his heart and stared right back at his cousin. 'I swear, I've been all about calculating the angular momentum. If I don't pass, my mum'll ground me, which means minimal hero time and zero Julie time. You do the math.' He looked down at the notebook, just as Julie had done. 'Because apparently I can't.'

'I believe him,' said Kevin, almost at once. He nodded at Ben. 'When you lie your left eye twitches. But who knows, maybe you've been blacking out and sleep-fighting.'

Gwen frowned. 'Is it possible? Is the Omnitrix making you attack your enemies in your sleep?'

Ben sighed and reached into the food wrapper. It was empty. 'If we're going to discuss this,' he mumbled, standing up, 'I need more chilli fries.'

CHAPTER TWO

FACE-TO-FACE

Across town, the door of the Burger Shack fast food restaurant swung open with a loud creak. Diners were sat at every table, munching on burgers and chilli fries, and chatting happily. None of them even noticed the boy with the green jacket and the weird-looking watch walk up to the counter.

'You all disgust me,' snarled the boy. 'This place is dispicable.'

Anyone who knew him would swear the boy was Ben Tennyson, but there was something different about him. Something not quite right.

'This miasma you call food, it's foul-smelling, oily digestive preparation, everything reeks,' he said to nobody in particular.

On the other side of the counter the

assistant looked up from the fryers and held up a paper bag. Greasy oil marks had already begun to seep through the paper.

'Yeah,' he grunted. 'Probably the onions.'

The boy who looked like Ben snatched the bag and slammed some cash down on the counter. The assistant slipped the money into the till, then turned back to the fryers.

With a look of utter disgust on his face, the boy in the green jacket tore open the bag and peered inside. The sight and smell of the chilli fries made him feel sick.

'All the same,' he muttered, 'I find myself strangely craving the entire putrid experience. It must be in the DNA.'

Shaking his head, the boy reached into the bag, pulled out one of the fries, and stomped away from the counter, just as the front door swung open once again.

'Chilli fries,' said Ben, smiling at the assistant and handing him payment. 'My favourites.'

'Careful, kid,' said the assistant. 'Those double portions catch up with you.' As if to prove his point, the man slapped his bulging belly hard.

Ben frowned. 'Excuse me?'

'Friendly advice,' said the assistant with a shrug. He handed Ben a bag. 'Take it or don't.'

Outside the Burger Shack, Gwen and Kevin were sitting in Kevin's car, waiting for Ben. Gwen raised her head from her hands as the door swung open and Ben stepped out.

'Here he comes,' said Gwen.

Over by the door, Ben let out a loud burp and shook his head angrily. 'I sicken myself,' he muttered. 'Disgusting.'

After wiping his greasy hands on his jeans, Ben turned the control dial on the Omnitrix and slammed it down. A swirl of green energy wrapped itself around him, transforming him in to the moth-like alien called Big Chill.

'What the heck?' said Kevin, watching Big Chill launch himself up towards the sky. Kevin cranked the engine of his car, kicked down on the accelerator and sped after the flying alien's ghostly blue form.

Had Kevin looked in his rear-view mirror right at that moment he'd have seen the door to the Burger Shack open and a very familiar figure step out.

Ben wiped his mouth on his sleeve, smacked his lips together and looked around the carpark for the car. Only then did he spot it roaring off into the distance.

'Guys?' Ben mumbled. He hesitated for a moment then began to run after them. 'Hey, guys! Wait for me!'

It was no use. There was no way he was catching up with the car on foot. Luckily, he had another option.

'Big Chill!' he cried, using the Omnitrix's power to transform him. With a twitch of his legs and a flap of his wings, the alien set off after the speeding car.

EEEEEEEK!

Kevin's tyres screeched as he skidded the car to a sudden stop right in front of another Forever Knight castle. He and Gwen leapt out. Lasers tore through the air around them, but for once they weren't the ones being shot at.

A Forever Knight stood on the drawbridge of the castle, pumping blast after blast up into the sky. A dark figure soared above his head, easily avoiding the bright red blasts.

And then, without making a sound, Big Chill was standing behind the shooter. 'Where is Ben Tennyson?' he hissed. 'I need to know or you will die.'

The knight spun on the spot, desperately trying to raise his gun, but before he could get off a shot, Big Chill breathed. A cloud of frosty mist swept over the knight, encasing him instantly in a block of solid ice.

An energy blast exploded against Big Chill's back, making him cry out. The alien turned to find four more Forever Knights rushing towards him, their energy lances primed and ready to fire.

'Attack!' cried the largest of the knights, barrelling into Big Chill and pushing him backwards.

The other knights surrounded the alien, preparing to fire. Before any of them could squeeze their trigger, a flying kick from Gwen sent two of them crashing into each other.

With a roar, another of the knights raised his sword, swinging it swiftly towards the side of Gwen's head. A hand that seemed to be carved from living rock caught the sword's blade and snapped it in half. With a grunt, Kevin quickly slammed his stony knee against the knight's armoured chest, knocking him to the ground.

Another knight took aim with his energy lance, its muzzle pointed directly at Kevin.

'Uh-oh,' said Kevin, waiting for the strike.

KLAAANK!

A wave of pink energy ripped from Gwen's fingertips, lifting the knight off the ground and slamming him hard against the castle wall. Inside the armour, the knight gave a low moan, then quietly fell unconscious.

'Thanks, Gwen. I owe you one,' Kevin smiled, jumping to his feet.

A cold breeze hit Gwen on the back of the neck. She spun around, hands raised, in time to see Big Chill freeze the last of the knights with his ice-breath.

With the attacking knights taken care of, Big Chill turned to look at Gwen and Kevin. Gwen stepped closer, her eyes scanning the alien features of his face. Something didn't seem quite right.

'Ben?' Gwen said, softly. 'Are you feeling alright? You kind of took off without us back there. We were worried.'

'You,' spat Big Chill, springing forwards and catching Gwen by the shoulders. 'You know of Ben. Where is Ben?'

Turning back into his usual form, Kevin stepped up and pushed Big Chill back.

'I knew you'd snap eventually,' Kevin said, just as the alien let out a big belch of icy air. 'Phew,' he said, holding his nose. 'Those chilli fries sure do radiate some toxic fumes.'

'Ugh. I agree,' said Big Chill. 'Everything about this planet is vile.'

'Huh? Change back, Ben,' Gwen told him. 'Let's get you home.'

Big Chill paused for a moment, a smile playing at the corner of his lips. He adjusted the Omnitrix and a cloud of green smoke surrounded him. In a flash, he transformed back into human form.

'Yes. It is I, Ben Tennyson,' he announced, slowly. 'Now you can transport me back to my domicile. There are grave matters of a personal nature to which I, Ben 10, must attend to.'

Before Kevin had time to think of a wisecrack reply, another voice called down to them from above.

'Hey, there you are! Thanks a lot, guys,' said Big Chill, swooping in for a landing. 'You left me at the diner. You really know who your friends are ...'

Suddenly, Big Chill noticed the boy in the green jacket with Gwen and Kevin. He quickly transformed back into human form.

Ben stepped forward and stared hard at the stranger. It was like looking in a mirror.

'So, who's your good-looking friend, Kevin?' Ben asked.

The other Ben looked him up and down. 'So you must be Ben Tennyson? A most difficult creature to find. I must speak to you as a matter of urgency.' He bowed his head, briefly. 'Please, let me introduce myself at once. I am Albedo of the Galvan.'

'A Grey Matter, hey?' said Ben. 'You're kinda tall for a little Galvan.'

'I am the builder of the Omnitrix,' continued Albedo, ignoring the hand Ben held out for him to shake. 'And I must have it back.

'Your days as Ben 10 are at an end.'

CHAPTER THREE

ALIEN VS ALIEN

Albedo held out his hand. 'Remove your Omnitrix and return it.'

Ben pulled his arm back and clutched the watch to his chest. 'Wait, Albedo,' he said. 'I thought this was the only Omnitrix in the universe. And anyway, a guy named Azmuth built it.'

'Azmuth is a liar.'

'But the DNAliens. The HighBreed. I'm supposed to save the world with it.'

'It is incomplete and prone to catastrophic malfunction.'

Ben gave the Omnitrix a soft tap. 'Not lately. It works pretty well for me.'

'You have great luck,' Albedo insisted, 'or by now you would have ripped a hole in the fabric of the universe.'

Gwen stepped closer to her cousin. 'He could be a HighBreed trying to trick you out of it,' she warned him.

'Maybe,' said Ben. 'Why don't you show your face?' he asked his lookalike. 'It feels a little crazy, talking to myself.'

'If only I could,' said Albedo, and Ben could hear anger in his voice. 'I am stuck in a sticky, sweaty, noisy, hungry, hairy, smelly teenage human body, constantly craving chilli fries and scratching myself in places I suspect are inappropriate.'

'Wow,' Gwen muttered, 'he really is you.'

'You see, your DNA is encoded as the default in your Omnitrix,' Albedo explained. 'Mine synchronises across space and time with yours. Unfortunately, you have become my default as well.'

Kevin began to pace around the fake Ben. 'Well, which is it?' he demanded. 'Do you want the watch to fix it or to keep the universe from falling apart?'

'Both.'

'Since you built the Omnitrix, tell me how it comes off,' said Ben.

'Yes. I trust you are versed in the practical applications of eighth-dimensional quantum gravity monopole equations?' replied Albedo. Ben watched his copy's face very closely while he spoke.

'It really does twitch when I lie,' he said.

Kevin nodded. 'Told ya.'

Ben, Gwen and Kevin stood side by side, each of them folding their arms across their chest. Albedo looked from one to the other, realising they weren't falling for his tricks.

'Very well,' he growled. 'There are other ways to disarm you.'

With a flash of blinding green light, Albedo changed into Jet Ray. Flicking out his tail he sent Kevin sprawling to the ground.

Ben moved to catch his friend, but a pair of alien feet grabbed him by his shoulders and yanked him off the ground.

Gripping Ben tightly, the Albedo Jet Ray flew higher. He was pleased with himself. Snatching Ben away had been much easier than he thought.

Suddenly, he felt the boy become much, much heavier, and they began to lose height. He looked down to find the face of an enormous dinosaur grinning back up at him.

'Humungousaur!' roared the dino-alien.

Releasing his grip, Jet Ray let Humungousaur drop down into the moat. The force of the dinosaur's landing sent water spraying higher than the castle itself.

Humungousaur bobbed his head up from below the water just as twin beams of green energy streaked down from the sky. Jet Ray swooped closer, firing blast after blast at the soaking-wet alien.

Throwing an arm up in front of his face for protection, Humungousaur dug the fingers of his other hand into the closest of the castle's stone walls. Tightening his grip, he flexed his muscles and launched himself up the wall, kicking with his feet and scrabbling with his hands until he made it all the way to the roof.

Another blast hit him in the face, spinning him around on the spot. 'That really stings!' he growled.

Breaking off a chunk of rock, Humungousaur hurled it up towards Jet Ray.

The flying alien dodged it easily. 'You are not worthy to wear the Omnitrix,' Jet Ray cried, arcing around and flying straight for the big dino-alien.

KERUUNCH!

Flying at full speed, Jet Ray slammed into Humungousaur. Already groaning beneath Humungousaur's weight, the castle roof gave way, and both aliens tumbled together into the gloomy darkness below.

Still out on the drawbridge, Gwen had been watching the battle with growing horror. 'Find something to touch,' she said, her voice shrill with panic.

Kevin frowned. 'Huh? Oh!' He reached down and picked up a fallen sword. There was barely enough metal in it to allow him to cover one arm. 'It'll have to do,' he said, and he and Gwen made their way inside the castle.

Humungousaur lay half-buried beneath what had once been the castle roof. He groaned with pain, but managed to open his eyes and shrug off most of the fallen rock. A shadow loomed over him.

'Thank you for your sacrifice,' hissed Jet Ray. His eyes began to glow green, ready to deliver the killer blast.

THWACK!

A rock bounced off Jet Ray's head.

'Ow!'

Another rock hit him, harder this time. Jet Ray turned to see Kevin take aim with a third boulder. The metal arm wasn't good for much, but it made throwing easier. Still, Kevin couldn't believe he was reduced to lobbing stones. He'd much rather be in the thick of the battle. 'What a crock,' he muttered.

Jet Ray moved to defend himself, but an enormous hand clamped down over the entire top half of his body. He tried to struggle, but his arms were pinned tightly in place.

'Give up,' boomed Humungousaur, as Jet Ray fired wildly with his eye lasers. 'I'm much better at this!'

A stray shot from Jet Ray slammed against the castle wall. Kevin looked up to see several tonnes of masonry come plummeting towards him. He couldn't tear his eyes away from the falling rocks, and it was only the sudden appearance of a pink energy shield that saved him.

Humungousaur relaxed his grip for a split-second as he watched Gwen and Kevin leap to safety, but it was all the time Jet Ray needed. Twisting hard, the red and yellow alien wriggled free, and streaked off upwards to be swallowed up by the dark night sky.

'He won't get far,' Gwen said, letting her fingertips brush against the spot on the drawbridge where Albedo had stood earlier. Her powers meant she could sense the energy given off by all living things, and Albedo was no exception.

She could follow it, like a trail. Albedo's mana energy would lead them right to him. And then they would find out his plan and they would stop it.

Once and for all.

CHAPTER FOUR

FOAM PARTY

Kevin's car prowled along another motorway, weaving through the last of the evening traffic. Gwen sat in the front passenger seat. She held a chunk of pink glowing rock in her hands, and was using it to track Albedo.

In the back, Ben leaned his head against his hand and stared glumly out of the window.

'So, evil twin, huh?' said Kevin, glancing

at Ben in the rear-view mirror. 'Guess you really are a hero – people want to be you.'

'Yeah, a hero with a big physics test in the morning,' Ben sighed. 'And I'd have been home studying if you'd have listened to me in the first place.'

'But who knows what damage Albedo will be doing if we don't track him down?' replied Gwen, before a shimmer of energy shook her hands. 'Turn here!' she cried.

Kevin twisted the steering wheel, pulled up the handbrake, and slid the car sharply around the corner.

The car's engine roared as it sped along a narrow road and into the carpark of a large factory. Ben, Gwen and Kevin pushed open their doors and stepped out, only to be met by dozens of screaming factory workers.

'Help! Monster!' shrieked one of the workers, as they ran past the car. 'It ate through the loading dock!'

Ben glanced at his companions, briefly nodded his head, then they all set off for the front door of the factory.

Inside, the factory was a mess. Computer terminals lay smashed on the floor, among a tangle of broken keyboards and exposed power cables. A bead of sweat formed on Gwen's brow as she fought to keep her concentration. But it was no use. With a flicker, the glowing rock went dim and dropped to the floor.

'It's impossible. There are too many machines here and not enough living things,'

Gwen grumbled. 'I can't track Albedo.'

'We'll have to split up,' Ben suggested. 'Let's see if we can surround him. We can't let him escape again.'

Gwen raised an eyebrow. 'How will we know which one's the real you?'

Kevin had already come up with a solution to that problem. Picking up a marker pen from a nearby desk, he drew a large black cross on Ben's cheek.

'Hey!' complained Ben.

'We'll call you Ben X,' replied Kevin, grinning from ear to ear.

Spitting onto his thumb, Ben wiped the pen mark away and gave Kevin an angry glare. Then, without another word, he headed off into the depths of the factory, leaving Kevin and Gwen to set off in the opposite direction. If Albedo was in here, they'd find him.

Over by a stack of wooden crates, a glowing green sludge oozed its way between the boxes and down onto the floor. The alien Goop wriggled and squirmed as he pulled himself into his normal shape, before a bright flash of green energy transformed him back into his human form.

Gwen and Kevin crept around the huge crates to find Ben standing just a few metres ahead of them. 'Guys,' he whispered. 'Come over here, I think I've found just what we've been looking for.'

Kevin narrowed his eyes. 'Hey, didn't you go the other way? How do we know that it's really you?'

'Well, um,' the boy said, uncertainly. 'Oh, man, I should not have erased that cross you drew on my face.'

With a nod of his head, Kevin agreed. Together, he and Gwen walked between the stacks of crates to where Ben had been pointing. They didn't notice him duck behind a pile of boxes, a wicked smile stretching his lips.

'Hit the deck!' cried a voice from much further along the corridor.

Kevin and Gwen whipped around to see Ben way off in the distance, running towards them. But if Ben was back there, then that meant ...

Albedo jumped out from behind the pile of boxes. He was pointing a large red hose right at Kevin and Gwen. Cackling with laughter, Albedo yanked open the nozzle lever. A powerful stream of thick, gloopy foam splurted out from the hose. It hit Kevin and Gwen at the same time, coating them from their necks all the way down to their feet.

'Woah!' Kevin shouted, trying to fight against the stinky foam. 'What's going on?'

By the time the Ben imposter switched the hose off, the foam had set hard. Their heads were the only parts of Kevin and Gwen still visible, everything else was well and truly stuck beneath the rock-solid foam.

'This reeks,' groaned Kevin, struggling to free himself. 'He got us with packing foam. There's no leverage.'

Gwen tried breaking free, too, but the hardened foam gripped them both too tightly. No matter how hard they pushed, there was no way of breaking free.

'Ben!' Kevin called over. 'Get us out of this disgusting stuff!'

Ben looked at Kevin and Gwen, and then back to Albedo.

'Look, Albedo, you're never going to get

my Omnitrix,' said Ben, being careful to stay out of range of the hose. 'Just let them go. You know I can kick your butt.'

'Aha, but what you haven't yet learned is that I have all of your powers, Ben Tennyson,' Albedo smirked, 'and a far superior intellect. You have no choice. You must surrender, if you value your life.'

'Oh, really? Why? Because that would be so much smarter,' sneered Ben, slowly reaching down for the Omnitrix.

SLAM!

Ben's hand came down hard on the watch, triggering another incredible transformation.

Every part of him – his skin, his hair, his bones – seemed to melt into a big puddle of glistening green, before forming into a tall, vaguely human-looking shape.

'Goop!' chirped the slimy alien, flexing his goo-like muscles.

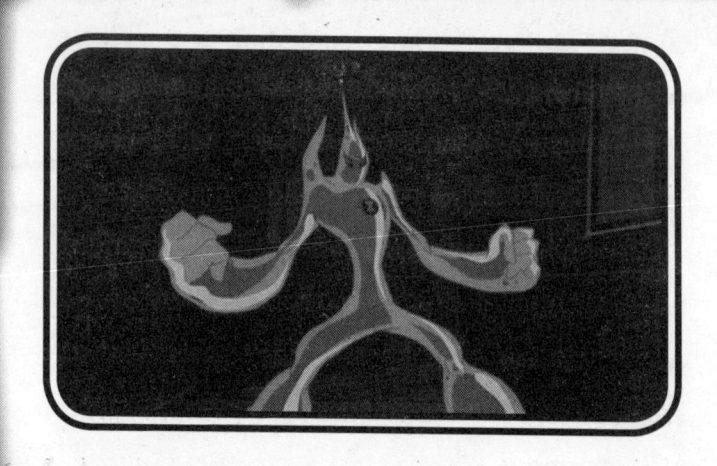

Roaring with anger, Albedo opened the nozzle of the hose and blasted a stream of stinky foam towards the alien. Goop swiftly leapt upwards, changing shape in mid-air a dozen times as he avoided Albedo's shots.

Raising a squidgy arm, Goop splattered the floor around Albedo with toxic green slime. The goo hissed noisily as it burned through the warehouse floor like acid. Albedo soon realised that packing foam was no longer going to cut it as a weapon. Luckily for him, he had a much more powerful weapon up his sleeve.

With a flash of light, Albedo struck

his own Omnitrix and transformed into the towering Humungousaur. Raising a tree-trunk leg, the dinosaur alien kicked a shelving unit, sending it hurtling towards Goop. The metal shelf-edges sliced straight through the alien's gooey body. Goop dropped to the floor in many different pieces. He flopped around wildly for a few seconds, then he quickly pulled himself back together.

Looking up, Goop saw Humungousaur crashing along the corridor towards him. Hitting the Omnitrix emblem on his chest he quickly transformed once again.

'Swampfire!' he cried, leaping up to his feet and throwing himself sideways just as Humungousaur's tail smashed down on the spot where he'd just been.

'Hey, big guy! Here's some mud in your eye!' shouted Swampfire, hurling handfuls of his own toxic sludge at the dino-alien's face.

The mud burned at Humungousaur's

eyes, blinding him for a few seconds. He let out loud roar.

Swampfire took full advantage and hammered Humungousaur with fireballs, driving him back along the corridor.

Meanwhile, Gwen was determined not to miss another minute of the battle. Focusing all of her energy powers through her eyes, she began to shoot out pink lasers. The lasers were melting away the rigid foam surrounding her and Kevin.

'Ow!' Kevin yelped. 'Hot.'

'Sorry!' said Gwen. 'But just hold still. I am sure I can burn our way out of here! We've got to help Ben.'

Another fireball hit Humungousaur, and another, and another. Reeling, the giant alien fumbled for the Omnitrix. He activated it just as another of Swampfire's flame bolts rocketed towards him.

Just in time, Albedo switched from Humungousaur to Big Chill. Swampfire's burning fireballs passed harmlessly through him and exploded against the back wall of the factory.

Big Chill sucked air deep into his lungs. The air cooled rapidly inside his ghostly body, and when he opened his mouth again a cloud of ice cold breath blew all over Swampfire's raging flames.

The frozen air put out the alien hero's fireballs, but that wasn't all. As Big Chill continued to blow, Swampfire felt his arms and legs become stiff. He quickly tried to lift his feet, but they were frozen to the floor. He tried to move his hands, but he could no longer feel any of his fingers.

As a layer of thick frost formed over Swampfire's body, a terrible realisation struck him: he was freezing.

He was freezing to death.

CHAPTER FIVE

CONFISCATED

The cold bit at Swampfire, numbing his whole body. How long could he stand it? A few minutes? A few seconds? If he was going to survive, he had to do something – and fast.

Summoning all his strength, Swampfire forced one of his arms to move. All the while, Big Chill was firing more ice blasts.

'Must get free ...' Swampfire slowly muttered to himself.

Swampfire tried to lift his arm again. This time freezing ice covering his arm cracked under the force of his alien muscles. He managed to reach up to the Omnitrix emblem on his chest.

The change happened quickly. Swampfire grew shorter and wider. Extra legs sprouted from his side and a hard shell began to form around him.

'Brain Storm!' he cried, shaking off the last of the ice. 'Tremble before my electrolocutive power, you feckless facsimile'

The top of the crab-alien's shell lifted up, exposing his enormous pink brain. Yellow sparks of electricity flickered across the wobbly surface, before forming into a powerful lightning bolt. The lightning stabbed up at Big Chill, hitting him squarely on the chest.

Big Chill threw back his head and howled in pain as the electricity flowed through his body. His wings curled in around him and he fell towards the floor, but not before he slammed his hand against his Omnitrix.

It wasn't Big Chill who hit the ground, but six duplicates of the alien, Echo Echo, who had the power to make multiple copies of himself. Every one of them cried out in shock as they slammed against the floor, but they were quickly on their feet again and rushing to surround Brain Storm.

Brain Storm shot at them with more electrical blasts, but the little aliens moved too quickly, leaping and bounding this way and that, avoiding every lightning bolt.

Exhausted, Brain Storm stopped firing for a moment. The Echo Echo clones quickly gathered together and closed in around him, a menacing look on their faces.

'Surrender. Or die. Surrender. Or die. Surrender. Or die. Surrender. Or die,' they chanted over and over again, before opening their mouths wide and unleashing six sonic blasts at the helpless Brain Storm.

'Deucedly difficult to cogitate,' Brain Storm groaned, throwing up two of his crab arms for protection. With another arm, he tapped the Omnitrix. A green flash of light shone across the warehouse and yet another transformation began.

'Jet Ray!' Ben cried, flipping up into the air and out of the paths of the sonic blasts. Flicking up his giant tail, the flying alien blasted lasers at the Echo Echoes below, sending them running for cover.

'You can't keep this up! You are too weak. You will not beat us!' they yelled up at Jet Ray, as one of them triggered his Omnitrix. In a blinding flash of light, they merged back into one and the evil imposter became the mighty Spidermonkey.

This time it was Spidermonkey's time to put his mighty tail to use. Raising it high above his head he shot thick strands of webbing up at Jet Ray, sticking him to the ceiling.

Bouncing once on the floor, Spidermonkey leapt up to the ceiling, landing right beside the trapped Jet Ray.

'You have reached the end. Your Omnitrix will soon lose all of its power,' the eight-legged alien growled, hitting Jet Ray with a series of hard punches across the jaw.

'Yield. Yield. Yield!' he shouted, between punches. 'You cannot win.'

The pain was almost too much to bear, but there was no way Jet Ray was giving up that easily. A power blast from his eyes knocked

Spidermonkey back down to the floor, buying him a few seconds.

Squirming around in the rock-hard steel web, Jet Ray tried to pull a hand free from the web. It wouldn't budge.

'Come on, get free!' Jet Ray muttered, using all of his might to free himself.

With one last push, Jet Ray managed to get a hand free. He quickly slammed down on the Omnitrix.

"Let's get even with some lasers!' he shouted out, as a transformation started to take place. 'ChromaStone!'

The alien hero's body glowed white hot for a moment – long enough to burn away the steel webs. The factory shook loudly as his feet slammed down against the floor, throwing up a cloud of choking dust.

As the dust began to clear, Spidermonkey saw a huge shape running towards him. It was ChromaStone. He was charging forwards with his fists raised high up in the air. There was no time for Spidermonkey to move anywhere. He swallowed hard.

'Uh-oh,' he said. This was going to hurt.

Just before the impact, a brief burst of green light lit up the room. In ChromaStone's place stood Ben, his fists still raised but his confidence quickly fading. 'Uh-oh,' he muttered, realising that all of the transformations had exhausted the watch.

'Haha! Told you,' giggled Spidermonkey.

'You have drained your Omnitrix. Whereas mine will last ...'

Spidermonkey quickly flashed back into human form, to demonstrate his own watch was still working perfectly.

'You see, I don't need an Omnitrix to destroy you, Ben Tennyson. I can do this all on my own,' Albedo cackled. He lunged forwards, swinging with a fierce punch. Ben did the same, throwing a punch of his own.

As the boys' fists passed each other they both cried out in shock. The Omnitrixes fizzed and sparked, pulling together like two powerful magnets. With a faint click they locked in place, trapping Ben and Albedo together.

'Aaaghh!' Ben shouted, as the sparks fell onto his skin.

'Get off me!' Albedo shouted.

'Do you seriously think I want to be attached to you, wise guy?' Ben asked.

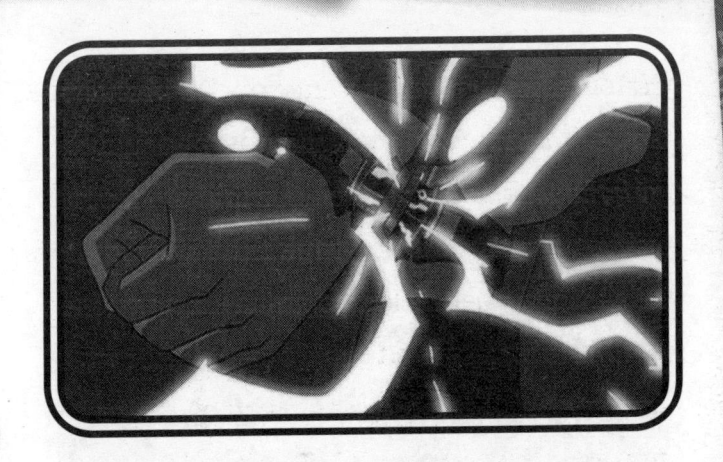

Albedo yanked hard, trying to pull away. Ben heaved his arm in the opposite direction, but they only succeeded in knocking themselves off balance. Albedo hit the ground first, with Ben falling on top of him. The Omnitrixes began to spark and crackle even more.

'What's going on?' Ben demanded. 'Are you doing this?'

'No. Their proximity is creating a bio-energy feedback,' Albedo replied, before one of the sparks hit him. A sudden change swept over the boy. His brown hair became as white as snow, while his green jacket turned the colour of dark, blood red.

'No confusing those two now,' muttered Kevin, who was still struggling with Gwen to be free of the foam.

The change caught Ben by surprise, allowing Albedo to flip him over onto his back. Now Albedo was pinning Ben to the floor.

'You have damaged this form,' Albedo snarled. 'You will pay.'

But Ben wasn't beaten yet. Twisting his body he managed to turn Albedo around and wrap an arm around his neck. 'Tell me how to get these apart.'

'Perhaps if one of us could manage to die.'

'Don't tempt me,' Ben growled.

Kevin groaned. Although Ben had Albedo in a choke-hold, he was still pinned to the wall. 'Great. Now we're all trapped.'

'Come on,' Gwen urged, firing up her eye beams. 'One more.'

Flexing his muscles, Kevin pushed against the foam as Gwen hit it with an energy blast. With a loud crack the hardened foam split open!

They rushed along the corridor just as Ben and Albedo struggled back to their feet, still fighting. A shower of green sparks exploded from inside the joined Omnitrixes. Then, to Ben's surprise, the watches separated all on their own. He looked up at Albedo and immediately saw the panic in the boy's eyes.

'He's here,' Albedo whispered.

'Who's here?'

'Azmuth.'

'You bet he is!' said a tiny alien, teleporting in. He craned his neck to look up at the humans. 'Azmuth of the Galvan, the true genius behind the Omnitrix.' He turned his gaze on Ben. 'You've overloaded the thing so badly I could sense it half a galaxy away. Those non-stop transformations are gonna break it.'

'I was just – '

'Save it. I know. Albedo, my former assistant, built an inferior copy.' He glared at Albedo. 'I warned you that there could only be one Omnitrix. You ignored me.'

'Someone's in trouble,' said Kevin, quietly.

'I will not trust the universe's fate to an unworthy human such as Ben Tennyson,' Albedo snapped. 'If my Omnitrix cannot function, then I will have his.'

'I told you, the Omnitrix is beyond you. You could have doomed us all.'

'So the universe really was at stake?' asked Ben, shocked.

'If you'd lost the Omnitrix, yes. Albedo only wanted it to restore his original form.'

'This human body is simply unbearable,' Albedo explained.

'I get that,' Kevin nodded. 'And the face is even worse.'

'Albedo, through your arrogant act of rebellion, you have proven yourself a lesser being,' said Azmuth. Leaping up, he removed the dial of Albedo's Omnitrix. 'You shall remain as you are, in a prison of your own making.'

'No! You can't!'

Azmuth nodded. 'I have.'

A flickering light surrounded Albedo
and he began to teleport away. 'I hate you!' he
screamed, before he vanished completely.

'He won't bother you again,' said Azmuth.

'I still have a few questions,' said Ben.
'Like, what's the watch really for? And how
many aliens can I – ?'

'Look, kid. You alone have made the
Omnitrix a force for good, in ways I'd never
conceived. It's better to allow you to create
your own way of using it.' He hopped up onto

Ben's hand. 'For all my concerns, you're the only being worthy to wear it. And I'm not the only one who thinks so.'

'Who else?'

Azmuth smirked. 'It's a surprise.'

'Now you're just teasing,' said Kevin.

A shimmering light began to surround Azmuth and he began to fade. 'There are difficult times ahead,' he said. 'Be ready.'

And with that, the three heroes were alone in the empty factory. Ben wasn't sure he liked the sound of Azmuth's last words, but right now he had bigger things to worry about. He had a Physics test in just a few hours – a test he had barely done any studying for.

Azmuth's warning didn't matter, he decided. If he could pass the Physics test then everything would be fine. After all, if he could get through that, he could get through anything.